I0619336

As a Mere Breath

Short Stories

Markus McDowell

Keledei
PUBLICATIONS

An Imprint of Sulis International Press
Los Angeles | Dallas | London

ISBN (print): 978-1-958139-63-9
ISBN (eBook): 978-1-958139-64-6

Published by Keledei Publications
An Imprint of Sulis International
Los Angeles | Dallas | London

www.sulisinternational.com

Other Fiction by Markus McDowell

To and Fro Upon the Earth: A Novel

Onesimus: A Novel of Christianity in the Roman Empire

The Sky Over Chaos: Short Stories

Mortals As They Walk

So Deep in Shadow: Short Stories

Nuff Sed: A Novel of Desert Steve

Contents

You have made my days a few handbreadths,
*   and my lifetime is as nothing in your sight.*
Surely everyone stands as a mere breath.

—Psalm 39.5

FISHHOOKS

T he tiny, barbed hook slowly penetrated his skin, just below the surface. It slid through the upper layers of skin—deep enough to be more than a slight prick, but enough to embed the barb so it would not pull out. He could see that a line was connected to the hook's eye, which disappeared into the darkness ahead. Unable to discern its endpoint, he felt a slight tug. It hurt, but it was just a small fishing hook. He decided it would be more painful to remove it than let it stay. It would probably work itself out through time. He was pretty sure that happened with splinters, so it was likely the same.

He was startled when the second hook pierced his skin. It was the same size as the first, also with a line receding away. It was wisest to leave it undisturbed as well. There were slight tugs at the lines, almost imperceptible. It might just be his imagination. If he remained relatively still, he didn't feel any pain. It alarmed him a bit, but really, it was no problem. He was a bit curious about where the hooks were coming from, but that seemed irrelevant at the moment.

As subsequent hooks pierced his flesh, each with its own thin line, he became accustomed to the momentary pain. After all, it was the same thing as the first one, and it was fine. It was as if his flesh had become numb to the sensation. He contemplated pulling and yanking them out, but he knew *that* pain would be excruciating. Far worse than simply leaving them there. They weren't doing any damage once they were embedded.

Of course, he knew they couldn't remain forever. And maybe they would work themselves out. In any case, if they didn't, he would have more willpower later to perform the fearful work. Meanwhile, he found that he suffered more damage by struggling. It was not ideal to leave them, but it was acceptable and bearable. Something should be done. But not at the moment.

Time passed. He gained more hooks in his flesh. Some were slightly larger, and others went deeper than the previous. The initial pain didn't seem much worse, though. Or maybe he was getting used to it.

A particularly large barb caused him to cry out as it penetrated deep into his flesh. "I have to stop this!" he said aloud. But the sheer number of hooks now made any movement unbearable, as it would start ripping muscles, skin, and flesh. Even the thought of the damage and pain caused his heart to beat faster, and a cold sweat broke out. He tried to remain still, and that helped.

He began to realize that the slight increase in pain was because all the lines were pulling him toward the

2

darkness. Ever so slowly, just the slightest tug. He would move slightly forward—just a few centimeters—and the pain was gone. Until the next time. Just a tiny bit, a few millimeters, released the tension for a brief moment. Had that been happening all along, so imperceptibly that he didn't notice at first?

He tried to think of other things. He no longer even noticed when new hooks slid into the flesh. The slight pain and then movement feared simply became part of his life. Part of what he did.

There came a time—he did not know how long—when he looked at his body and was horrified to see hundreds of nasty, large, barbed hooks all over his body. The skin had healed and covered all around the hooks and barbs that had been there a while. They had become part of him, part of who he was.

Panic gripped him. *I am a dead man!* Attempting to rip himself free now would result in so much blood and gore that he was certain he would pass out. Perhaps he would die of blood loss. Yet, staying in this state was equally terrifying, for there were always more hooks, and the darkness was growing ever closer. For the first time, he wondered what was ahead.

It is hopeless. I am trapped. Oh, why did I not pull them out when they were only a few!

He began to believe that the unknown darkness might be worse than any pain he might experience. Part of his mind told him that death lie ahead, though he had no idea where that conclusion came from.

Somehow, from somewhere, he gathered strength. Escape from the hooks and impending doom, regardless of the cost, would be worth the pain, suffering, and damage. Even if he died in the attempt, he would at least die in freedom.

He steeled himself for an action that he was not certain he could do. If only someone could help him. But he had no one. He was alone. Perhaps if he had cried for help in the beginning...but now he was too far. Besides, he couldn't tell anyone—what would they think? How had he gotten into this predicament? How stupid can one be?

To move quickly seemed best, as slower movements just exacerbated the pain. If the pain increase too much, he feared he would stop and never be able to try again.

Fast. Quick. Don't think. Act.

With all the strength he could muster, he pulled in the opposite direction of the lines, yanking, spinning, and leaning back. The pain was excruciating, worse than he had imagined. His momentum carried him backwards. He broke out in a sweat. He screamed. He cried. He became dizzy with the agony. He thought he might faint.

Suddenly, he was free. He didn't even notice at first in the midst of all the torment. He stumbled and fell, collapsing onto the cold floor. He was a heap of tattered flesh. The throbbing pain permeated his body, and beneath it, he was aware of the warm, sticky sensation of blood.

He passed out.

When he regained consciousness, he sat up wounded, bleeding, exhausted, and dying. But he had made it! The pain was still overwhelming, almost causing him to lose consciousness. It didn't matter. He was free. He had done it. A glimmer of hope even felt within him. "If I survive this, I can start healing," he whispered to himself.

Recovery was arduous. The ragged and bleeding wounds kept reopening, and the damage was far worse than he had thought. A few people, seeing him writhing on the ground, rushed to help staunch the wounds. Others stood farther away, offering some comforting words. But most simply backed away in horror, or went on their way, pretending not to notice. To his puzzlement, some stood a way off and mocked him. One said, "What a pathetic man—that would never happen to me." Another responded with, "Just leave him there to die—he deserves it."

He was surprised to discover how deeply the hooks had been embedded and how many there were. Many wounds were larger and more ragged than he had anticipated. He thought some of the wounds would never stop bleeding. At times, he looked at his tattered body and did not think he would survive recovery. *These are mortal wounds.*

It would be such a relief to simply give up, lay down, and let the pain and suffering take him into a restful death. He could die with the knowledge that he had triumphed over the darkness.

Although he survived the initial trauma, he did not know if he would survive the aftermath. Would the wounds ever stop bleeding? If they did, would the scars be so ugly and repulsive that he would be an outcast forever? Would the scar tissue hinder him the rest of his life—however long or short that might be? He could not imagine ever being whole again.

Still, freedom counts for something, doesn't it?

YOU MADE YOUR BED...

The bed complained, its frame over fifty years old. The mattress, box springs, and bedclothes were equally aged, though not as old as the frame. Well-worn to the point of comfort, they were still structurally sound and aesthetically pleasing. However, its age was evident in its style and the way it creaked as the owner stirred restlessly.

The occupant shifted, rolling over to the side closest to the nightstand. A soft, well-worn creak echoed through the room. It wasn't an unpleasant sound; rather, a comforting, homey creak, reminiscent of the floorboards of an old, cozy house, bearing the signs of a life well-lived.

The alarm blared—a stark contrast to the rustic groan of the bed. A groan escaped the man lying there. With a deep sigh, he pushed himself to a sitting position and reached over to silence the alarm. Three distinct parts of the bed squeaked in unison, causing the structure to sway slightly as he swung his legs to the side and stood up. He took a deep breath, turned, and looked at the covers. *I need to make the bed. I don't think I've done it in a week,* he muttered. He stood there for a moment, eyes half-closed. *I'll do it after I eat something,* he decided.

✦

After breakfast, he stepped into the adjoining bathroom for a shower. A patch of autumn sunlight streamed through the large, curtain-less window, slowly making its way across the floor towards the bed. By the time he emerged from the shower, the light had climbed half-way up the footboard. If he had looked, he would have noticed the years of work the sunlight had done on the wood surface: the uneven fading, the thinning, or disappearance of the varnish, and the cracks and scrapes on areas that had dried out and been neglected.

He returned to the room, fastening his watch to his wrist. He realized the hour was late. His cat sauntered in from the hallway. "Ah, I need to feed you before I leave! Late again," he muttered. He grabbed the pillows and tossed them at the headboard, then straightened them out. *Damn, I don't have time for this. Tonight when I get home, I'll just make it a chore and change the sheets. How long has it been? Maybe five or six days.* He rushed out of the room.

The room was dark as he moved slowly through the door and switched on the lamp beside the bed. The room lit up. *Ah! I was going to change the sheets tonight!* He paused. *Where's the other set? Have I washed them yet?* He tossed the plastic bag he was holding on to the bed. Some items from the bag fell out onto the crumpled sheets: soap, a bottle of mouthwash, and a pack of razors.

Two hours later, he stumbled back into the room. He had gone downstairs to find clean bedclothes and found them in the dryer. While folding them and some other clothes, he got entranced in a basketball game and drank half a bottle of whisky. He fell asleep on the couch before the game ended and woke up with a start much later. He came upstairs, fell onto the bed, fumbled around with the covers, and was snoring in a matter of moments. Around 1:00 a.m., he awoke, stumbled to use the bathroom, returned, switched off the lamp, and fell heavily back into bed with a groan.

The alarm had been blaring for thirty minutes before he finally woke up. Another groan escaped his lips. He slowly rolled over to glance at the clock, but it took a few moments for his vision to clear enough to read the numbers. *Oh, damn!* he exclaimed, jumping up and getting tangled in the bedclothes. He crashed to the floor in a heap.

His head throbbed, his mouth felt sticky and gross, and his stomach grumbled in protest. *I have to stop doing this every night,* he muttered. Despite putting in countless hours at work and being exceptionally skilled at his job, he felt a sense of pride in his ability to come in late. He believed that taking responsibility and doing your best was what made a man valuable. He wasn't going to mess that up.

He untangled himself from the bedclothes and made his way to the bathroom, wincing with each step as the pain in his head intensified. After a few minutes, the shower was ready. When he emerged from the shower, he rummaged through the bedclothes and found the bag of items he had brought home the previous night. He struggled to open the sealed plastic bottle of mouthwash. Finally, he managed to get it open and took a sloppy swig. Some of the liquid spilled onto the edge of the mattress and the bedclothes, which were half on the floor.

"Argh!!" He shook his head violently, then winced at the pain. He set the open bottle down on the nightstand.

As he finished dressing, he noticed the room was quite warm. *Why is it so hot?* He flung open the French-style window, letting in a refreshing breeze from a crisp autumn morning. *Much better. Got to check the air conditioner this evening.* He leaned out the window, feeling the cool air caress his face and reaching out to touch the vibrant pine leaves from the large tree outside. They were fresh, alive, and inviting.

The house had been eerily silent and empty for hours. It was dusk, and the clear sky had transformed into a stormy canvas. Although the temperature had been cool all day, the weather had taken a turn for the worse as the afternoon wore on. The temperature dropped, and the autumn wind began to blow, swirling around the house and gusting through the open window.

The cat was curled up on the bed, oblivious to the impending storm. As darkness rapidly descended, the storm clouds grew thicker, obscuring the sun.

A few autumn leaves, caught in the wind, drifted into the room and landed on the bed and the floor. The cat jumped off the bed and dashed out of the room as the rain began to fall. If someone had been present to listen, they would have heard the pitter-patter of raindrops on the grass, sidewalk, leaves, and roof. The rain intensified.

The bed creaked as the occupant stirred. He had slept in again. He rolled over, glanced at the clock, and sighed. *Ah, Saturday. Wonderful sleep.* He rolled back over and pulled the covers over his head. A leaf fluttered to the floor.

The room bathed in the warm, golden light of the late afternoon sun filtering through the window. The sound of stomping feet echoed up the stairs as he came inside from working in the yard all day. With a loud thump, he sank onto the edge on the messy bed, letting out a deep, weary breath followed by a long, drawn-out sigh. *I am so tired,* he muttered, *and I don't feel well.*

He turned his head to catch a glimpse of himself in the mirror hanging above the dresser. His pale skin was covered in dirt and filth, and his cap, stained with grime and sweat, hung limply on his head. He removed it, revealing a dark, sweaty shirt that had been stained under his armpits from the strenuous work.

As he gazed down at his jeans, he noticed that water had seeped up into the fabric from the wet yard, leaving a dark stain from mid-calf down. The bottoms of each pant leg were caked in mud, making it impossible to see the hems. His boots were equally covered, and he observed that some of the unmade bedclothes had fallen to the floor, with one boot resting on top.

Dirt and mud balls clung to the sheet, and he lifted his foot, grimacing in disgust. *Ugh,* he groaned, *I really have to wash these sheets now.*

A wave of nausea washed over him, and he jumped up, rushing into the bathroom. He left behind boot-shaped mud prints. A few moments later, he emerged, wiping his mouth with a tissue.

He let out a groan, going downstairs to retrieve a box of crackers and a can of soda from the kitchen. Back upstairs, he eased himself onto the bed, swinging his feet up and bracing his back against the headboard. The wood protested under his weight, creaking as he pushed it back against the wall.

Ah! Boots! He laid aside the crackers and soda, and, with some effort, leaned forward, pulling his foot back towards his chest and removing both boots, tossing them onto the floor. He didn't notice the dirt and mud now covering himself and the sheets. Slumping back—*creak*—he popped open the can and drank. After a few sips, he opened the box of crackers and ate a few, but they were dry, making his mouth feel even sicker. He tossed the box aside and gulped down the rest of the soda. *Better. The carbonation helps. So tired. So hot.* He scrunched down to lie flat, then set the can on the bed beside him. It fell over, and the last bit of liquid seeped onto the bedclothes. He was already drifting off to sleep, breathing slowly and methodically.

✦

Monday morning arrived with an overcast sky, making it darker than usual. The alarm went off. The figure on the bed rolled over and silenced it. *Creak.* He lay still for a moment. *Better. My fever has stayed down since last night. Maybe I'm finally over it.*

After a few moments, he rose to a sitting position, disentangling himself from the bedclothes to sit on the edge of the bed. He took a slow, deep breath. *A whole Sunday in bed. More than twenty-four hours, just lying here.* He remembered the fever, the sweating, and throwing the bedclothes off, then the shivering and pulling them back up. *Have I eaten anything since Saturday night?* He didn't even remember getting up except to go to the bathroom. *Oh, yes, I went downstairs and made some tea early Sunday morning. And fed the cat. It feels like a distant dream.*

He leaned over and set the alarm for the last possible moment to still make it to work on time. He would skip breakfast. He lay back down and soon fell asleep again.

He leapt up as the alarm blared and stood there, momentarily bewildered. The moment of disorientation passed, and he glanced at the clock. It was okay; he had time. The memories returned: the fever, the sickness, the days spent confined to bed. Although still weak, he felt a sense of relief. He flung the bedclothes aside and cautiously made his way to the bathroom.

After washing his face, he returned to the bedroom and switched on the lamp beside.

"Oh, my God!" he exclaimed.

The bedclothes were in a state of disarray, resembling the intricate knots as if created by Gordian himself.

Half of the bed was covered in stains and dirt. *How long has it been since I changed them?*

A movement beneath the sheet startled him. The cat.

"What are you doing here? Didn't I put you out?" The creature, at the sound of his voice, wriggled out from her hiding spot and approached him. He shooed her away and noticed that she had used part of the bed as a litter box. He pulled the covers and sheet aside, revealing an empty can on the floor and leaves fluttering. The sheet underneath was just as dirty, with light and dark soiled spots scattered throughout. Crumbs of food, dirt, and unidentifiable liquids completed the mess. The cover sheet itself appeared to have been exposed to the elements for months. He let out a deep sigh.

Reaching down, he pulled the edge of the fitted sheet from the mattress and walked to the head of the bed, pulling it along. As the mattress was exposed, he saw that the dirt, spills, and excrement had seeped through as well. He dropped the sheet in despair. His eyes scanned the entire bed, as if seeing it for the first time. Even the wood frame, headboard, and footboard were stained and weathered. A sticky liquid had run down the footboard near the middle and dried. The wood was cracked and worn.

He stood there, puzzled by how his bed could be in such a terrible state. *Someone must have done this. Someone must have broken in. I did leave the window open a few days ago. Or was it last week. I haven't been here much; I've been working so hard. There's no way I would let it get to this point. I'll have to sleep downstairs tonight.*

He turned and walked towards the door. He paused for a moment, considering whether he should use the bathroom first. *I'll use the one downstairs,* he decided. He walked through the door, pulling it shut behind him, ensuring it latched securely.

TRAIN WRECK

There was no one in sight. Lino looked down the old road in the direction of Padova, from where he had just come. The Italian countryside stretched out all on sides, a pale green plain dotted with patches of yellow. It was silent. Nothing moved. It was cold. It was clear. A normal winter day in northern Italy.

He turned back in the other direction. His worn shoes made a grinding sound on the gravel, surprisingly loud in the stillness. He knew that ahead of him lay the town of Vicenza. A town he had never seen. He looked down the road. It appeared to be a mirror of the view behind him: a shabby pavement, stretching on into the distance. Pale winter farmlands spread out on either side. An occasional clump of trees and sections of old stone walls in the distance. To the right, the countryside rose slightly. At the top, far off, was what appeared to be a stone farmhouse and a barn. It could well be abandoned. Just ruins. Or it might be full of life in the midst of this cold, clear afternoon. From this distance, Lino could not tell. All seemed quiet and still.

Now he turned to his left, breaking the silence once again. Train tracks stretched away in this direction. A row of trees lined one side, an open field on the other. Telephone poles were standing on the right side of the track. Silent totems evenly spaced, each one down the line seeming to be smaller than the previous until they disappeared in the distance. A line of carefully planted trees functioned as a windscreen between each set of poles. At first glance, the scene had a very neat, ordered geometry. Two straight iron tracks, receding away until they touched. Wooden cross-ties layed at specific intervals under the rails. The evenly spaced telephone poles and trees. Lino counted the number of trees between the two poles closest to him. Thirteen. He counted the next set, and the next: as many as he could until the distance made it impossible to see. Thirteen each time.

Lino turned a fourth time. Crunch. Once again, a mirror of the opposite direction, except in the distance the tracks curved around rising hills, the line of trees hiding the poles after the curve. He could only count three poles (thirty-nine trees) from his vantage .

Standing in the middle of the street where the tracks crossed, Lino imagined what he looked like from far above. A small, insignificant dot, standing at the center of a cross made of wood, iron, and dirt. He raised his arms up from his sides. He knew that one of his arms was longer than the other, one was stronger than the other. His hair was combed to the side. The left pocket of his coat had some bread and cheese in it. An uneven geometric figure in the midst of the straight, ordered geometry. An unplanned flaw in the midst of the carefully planned crossing. "A strange disfigurement standing at the cross," he said out loud. His voice startled him. It sounded loud and rough, like the gravel at his feet.

Why is order so important? Why do people think everything must be neat and structured? Why not unordered? Why can't disorder have meaning too? Why can't the nasty and disheveled and dirty and chaotic also have a function? Is order significant because it gives a sense of security? The boundaries are clear. We know where one thing ends and another begins. Beginnings. Endings. Crucial.

He turned and walked to where the edge of the road ended, and the tracks left the asphalt and continued on their long, straight path. He looked closely at the iron of the left-hand rail. It was quite worn. Where one section of rail fitted to another, it was slightly uneven. The rivets were leaning outward and a bit loose. If someone didn't check this and fix it, eventually there would be a derailment. *How long?* Lino wondered. How long would this have to stay untended before it caused a disaster? How many trains would go by, loosening the rivets a tiny bit each time, until it crossed that line between safety and disaster? He imagined a train, speeding along at 187 kilometers per hour. All the passengers (the lucky ones in *prima classe*) on just another run, just another trip, just another day. Suddenly, a bang! and a lurch! and rending and crashing and screeching. Which car would be the last to cross before all hell broke loose? Which person would be seated furthest back in that particular car? The last lucky one, who might never know how close he or she was to maiming or even death?

A sudden rustling off to the right disturbed his thoughts. He looked towards the sound. An animal in the brush. A bird or a rat. Lino stepped out onto the wooden cross-ties of the track. It was firm beneath his feet. He walked forward between the rails and stood on the next cross-tie. A third. A fourth. On the seventh, he stopped and bent down. He looked at the gravel piled between the cross-ties. All about the same size. The same grayish color. He picked up a handful, felt their coldness. He squeezed his palm. Stone edges dug into his hands and fingers. He turned his hand upside down and slowly released his grip until they began to drop, a lithic drizzle. *Where did all these come from? Are they made especially for this purpose? Is there a factory somewhere that turns these out? Each one, made for this function. They have a purpose. Maybe someone checks them all for quality assurance characteristics. Then someone packages them in large crates and ships them off. Someone else places them between the ties. Not too many, not too few. Everything according to a plan. Everything worked out ahead of time. Nice and neat.*

Lino looked to the side and saw one of the rocks off to the side of the rails, lying in the dirt at the bottom of the brief incline, built to raise the tracks two or three feet or so. *Ah! A rebellious rogue stone! Or a misfit!* He stepped across the iron rail and slid down to the rock. Now he stood on dirt. Around him were some brown weeds with a few bits of green poking up here and there. He stopped before the lone rock. How did it get out here? Did an animal pick it up and then drop it? Maybe the snow and the rain of the past winter had changed the configuration of rocks piled between the ties, and a speeding train flew by, causing it to careen off into the hinterland, no longer a part of the carefully ordered train-track universe. It was just a plain rock now. Lino bent down and picked it up. Perhaps, when they were laying the gravel, or re-laying, it simply slipped off the pile and rolled down here. Maybe a worker tossed it over here for fun. Possibly it had some defect that only a carefully trained locomotive industry specialist would note.

Lino wondered what difference it made that it was *here* and not *there*. It no longer performed its function. If it ever had. Now, it was just a rock. Not even a real rock. A manufactured rock, a pseudo-rock Made for some purpose, but served that purpose no longer. It didn't belong here with the *real* rocks and pebbles.

Still holding it, he looked down the tracks. About fifteen or twenty meters further along, there was a low concrete wall on one side of the track. He had not noticed it before. How did it fit into the order of the transportation system? There was no road crossing at that point. He began walking toward it, curious. Briefly, he wondered why he was curious. What difference did it make?

He arrived and observed that the wall, about ten meters long, had been built because a small stream ran under the tracks. The wall held back the piles of dirt and gravel which made up the rail bed. A corrugated culvert ran through the wall and under the tracks to some point beyond the other side that he could not see. How nice and neat. Just a long, large pipe, buried under the rails, with a wall to keep the bank steady. When the rains come, when the snows melt, the drainage can flow as if tracks had never bisected this part of the land. The trains could still speed across the plain, and the passengers need never know that a stream bisected their path.

He looked at his watch. He took a deep breath of the air. It was slightly warmer now, as the day progressed, but it still had that cool, crisp feel that almost hurt his lungs. He turned his head and listened. So silent. Not for long, though. He knew that the stillness would soon be broken by a deep and steady whooshing, and a clacking of metal on metal that would build in volume. The EC 86 Eurocity was due soon. He had ridden that train several times. No smoking was allowed—it did not even have a smoking car like most trains. Some passengers would complain about that, but Italians were getting used to it. There was a *Bordrestaurant* where one could buy pricey snacks, drinks, beer, and wine. It made many, many stops between the old, messy, stone-lined Venezia Santa Lucia train station on the Grand Canal and the modern, clean, metal-edged München station, its final destination.

He stepped up onto the top of the wall with some effort: it was over a meter high, and Lino was tired and hungry. He almost lost his balance, but he caught himself by waving his arms. Balanced, he turned and looked across the tracks. This new perspective offered no new insights, except that he could see where the culvert exited, about ten meters past the other side of the rails.

He noticed he still had the rock in his hand. The poor, misfit rock. He looked at the tracks below him. If he tossed it down, right there, it could land right between the ties. If he then looked away and then back, he probably wouldn't be able to find it. Returned to its world, it would fit in among its brothers and sisters, one among many, performing its duty without drawing any attention. A nice, orderly existence. Just what is expected of railroad gravel.

Of course, his aim might be off. Maybe a funny bounce would cause it to careen off the track again. *Ha!* thought Lino, *what an irony that would be. Just when you thought all was well, back to normal, and order restored—you are right back where you were moments ago.*

Perhaps it would bounce onto the cross-tie. Sitting there, on the wood. So obviously out of place. Naked to the world. Maybe the train would come by, and the incredible speed would expel the rock. Maybe it would crack and break up into unrecognizable pieces scattered about. It would have begun with a purpose in some factory somewhere, and ended as small pebbles strewn about with no purpose. Beginnings and endings. Significant.

He balanced the stone, ready to toss it. What would happen? Once again, his curiosity surprised him. Why did he care? It was a rock, one among thousands—millions! Still…

The sound caught his attention. The train was approaching. He looked to his left, and could already see the top of the engine. It was a long way off, but he knew how fast it was moving. The sound grew louder, a terrible dragon roaring and speeding along, destroying everything in its path, a mighty metal monster with a tail made of a twisting windstorm.

He threw the rock as hard as he could over the tracks without losing his balance. The concrete began to tremble beneath his feet, and he lost sight of the rock. It must have travelled quite a distance from the tracks. It would probably never be seen again by anyone. He was the last to see it, to hold it, to give it a thought.

He did not look, but by the sound, he knew the train had almost reached the road crossing. A beast of enormous power bearing down on him. It would pass him within seconds.

He closed his eyes. Beginnings and endings. So vital.

The *controllore* inserted his key into the lock of the communications panel, smooth and swift. He opened the thin metal door and swung it open. Lifting the phone off the hook and, he used the top of the receiver to flipped the switch labelled "all cars." He pulled a notebook out from under his right arm with his left hand and glanced at the page. He raised the phone to his mouth and clicked the button on the phone, knowing that, at that moment, all passengers on every car would stop whatever they were doing to listen.

"*Buon giorno*, may I have your attention? We have stopped because the train has struck something. There is no damage to our train, but we must wait until the Polizei arrive to make the report. Once this is done, in about an hour, we will be on our way to Vicenza. The *Bordrestaurant* is open for your convenience. We apologize for this brief interruption in your travels. Grazie."

MOTIVATION NULL

H e sat in the small cubicle facing the computer screen. His elbows were on the desk, his hands cradling his face. Staring at the screen. *Code. I need to code. Two days until the deadline. Type. Type!*

Nothing. He would rather be anywhere than here. Even at the hospital for surgery. At least it wouldn't be here, day after day, staring at the screen. Soon the deadline would come. The code would be due. The project manager expects it, so he could then take that code and make it part of the rest of the code from other programmers, and complete this part of the project so they could start testing the program. Everyone else was writing furiously. No one ever complained how much they hate it.

I hate programming! He screamed the words in his head.

No, I don't hate programming. I love it. I have always loved it. Since I was a kid, playing with my dad's computer. Programming. Coding. Making graphics, making text appear on the screen. It was like being God. I cre-

ate something from nothing. Words, symbols, diagrams. Programming is both science and art. They come together to produce something meaningful, something useful, or something entertaining.

Maybe I don't like programming. Perhaps I only thought I did. Maybe I have been deluding myself all along. Maybe, all my life, I only liked the idea *of being a programmer. Maybe actually being one was not what I wanted to do, or was even good at.*

He recalled that day he realized that he didn't like omelets. He loved the *idea* of an omelet. The eggs broken into the special skillet. All the possible ingredients to add. Cheese, onion, sausage. Each element is added at the proper moment in order to make a perfect omelet. The exacting use of the spatula to create the slowly hardening egg mixture. The expert twist of the spatula to fold the omelette in on itself. The expert flip of the skillet to make the half-moon shape. The well-practiced slide that moves the omelet onto the plate. There sat the omelet, a wonderful and skillful construction of egg, cheese, and vegetables, folded and molded into a nice, neat package. But he didn't *really* like the taste. He didn't like the slightly toasted edge of the egg and the soft middle. Scrambled eggs, he liked. Hard-boiled eggs, good stuff. But for some reason, he just did not like the taste of omelets.

Maybe it was the same with programming. He didn't honestly like programming or being a programmer. Only the concept of being a programmer was attractive to him.

No, that wasn't true, was it? He did like sitting at the computer, programming. The freedom, the self-discipline, the work of the individual who contributed to the whole. The creation. And he *was* good at it. That's the reason he was hired. They had interviewed hundreds of programmers, and they had chosen only three. He was offered the second position. Second out of hundreds. Pretty good.

So what was the problem? Why couldn't he write? It wasn't that he couldn't do it. It was that he didn't want to. No desire. No urge. No interest.

A break. I need a break.

He stood up from his chair and stretched. Turning, he looked around in the opposite direction of his desk, across the tops of the cubicles. Typical. Just like every office scene in every TV show and movie. A big room, divided into office cubicles with partitions about five feet high. He could see the tops of heads, parts of large plastic plants sticking up. A few desk lamps. Books on top of shelves.

He became aware of the sounds. The clicking of computer keyboards. A few voices in the distance talking quietly, not loud enough to hear distinct words. The soft whooshing of the air conditioning.

He looked up. Florescent lighting. He hated fluorescent lights. They covered the room in a dull, empty, grayish light. The off-white color of the walls, the off-white color of the cubicle partitions, and the white panels of the drop ceiling all gave the impression of a clean, but lifeless, space. Fluorescent lights sucked the life out of everything. Those glass tubes sprayed living beings and materials with a wave of light that sapped it all of its verve, its color, its vivaciousness.

Maybe that was his problem. The environment. He turned around and switched on his large desk lamp. It was incandescent. That's why he had bought it. But he rarely turned it on. There was a plant sitting on his desk. He moved it nearer the computer screen. If he could see some life, feel the heat of *real* light as he wrote, this would enliven him. Good. Yes.

A coffee cup sat next to the keyboard: coffee. Coffee. A shot of caffeine was always good to get started in the morning, but maybe something more fresh, more alive, is what he needed. He pulled a bottle of water from his bag sitting on the floor and twisted the cap off. Tilting it up, he took a long, slow drink. Ah. Yes. Living water. Clean, clear, fresh. The essence of life.

Now he was ready. He sat back down, moved his chair to make it more comfortable, and placed his hands on the keyboard. First, he required the opening and closing code; the headers first. He typed. These were codes he had typed over and over, so many times. Standard lines of code. Good. The main structure is there. Now, code the rest of the structure of this particular section. He had been thinking about it so long, this was easy to do. Five major sections of code. He typed them up, the comment lines showing him where each section began. Markers with comments to show where, eventually, all the actual code would be. Good. Once this was done, he could then begin working on each of the sections. Of course, each would consist of hundreds of lines, more specific, more detailed, and would take a lot of concentration, creativity, and just plain work. The structure was easy. Now he'd have to consult a number of his reference books. And he'd have to run parts of it within the shell to check it to make sure he hadn't missed anything and there were no errors.

Okay. It felt good to have done something. The structure is in place. He should be much further along, but at least he had something. Now he could see what was left. Fill in the parts.

Yes. Okay. First section. Now, it might help to comment the subsections. Get an idea of the smaller structure within the larger structure. Hm…

He came to with a start. How long had he been thinking? He had drifted. Thinking about last night, thinking about getting off work and going to the grocery store, thinking about the grocery list. Would he try to work some more on the program at his apartment? Actually, if he could get something done today, feel good about it, even if he was still behind, that would be a small victory. Maybe he could then feel good about rewarding himself tonight. No pressure to work. Watch a movie. Maybe go to bed early. Maybe more sleep would give him the boost to make tomorrow more energetic for him, and he'd then be able to make up time.

He was doing it again. He was not working. *Ah! What is the problem? Why can't I do this?* Why was there no interest in his chosen profession, his chosen work? All his friends, all his acquaintances, his family, found it so interesting that he was a computer programmer. No need to wear a suit and tie. He could dress however he wanted. He could take off early and work at home. He could take his laptop and work at a park or a coffee shop. He got paid a lot of money. Doing what he loved. There was even a mystique about it: all those symbols and code and terminology shared by "technology geeks." It was like a secret society that everyone depended on because everyone used computers. *We are like the priests of a technological society. The druids of an advanced age. We hold the knowledge, the skills, and the mystique. Come to us, and we will help you and show you the way. You won't understand it, but our mediation will benefit your life.*

With a start, he slammed his hand on the desk and spun around. He did it again. What was the problem?

A head popped up above the partition beside him. "You okay?"

He looked up. "Yeah."

"Did you crash?"

"No. Just stuck on a line here I can't get past." Realizing that the line of sight would enable his neighbor to see the screen and the fact that there was no real code, he moved over slightly, trying to be casual, to block the screen.

"Well, why don't you go for a walk? It's almost lunch. Take an early break. Clear your head. That works for me."

"I don't know. Maybe."

His neighbor shrugged, and the head disappeared.

How embarrassing. Why did he say that? Why not just say, "I am seriously blocked. I haven't written a thing on this section of code, and I don't know how to get past it?" Why not ask for help? Surely other programmers have been through this. In fact, he knew they had. He had heard others say so.

But those were not the good programmers. They were average, with moments here and there of brilliance. The genius coders, the high priests, the Chief Druids—they never talked about difficulties with motivation. Programming code flowed from their brains like beer from a newly filled tap. They lived, breathed, and ate code.

He used to be like that. It was so easy. It just flowed, rich and full. Now, it was hard work. And it seemed there was nothing there. Nothing. Maybe that was it. He was used up. He only had so much code in him, and he had used it up. Now, the cup is empty. The tank is dry. He did great work before, but now it's all over.

No, that's silly. That isn't the way it works. There aren't "so many words in an author," or "so many paintings in a painter." It is what they did. It wasn't a reservoir, it was their work, training, and talent.

He leaned back in his chair. Maybe he needed to eat better. Or get more sleep. Or maybe he needed to find some new inspiration and find his heart again.

Maybe going to lunch was a good idea. This certainly wasn't getting him anywhere. Though he did get something on the screen. Look at that. The screen is ready to go. He did work.

Oh, don't kid yourself. That is preparation, not substance. A monkey could have done that. Someone could have copied that part out of an elementary codebook.

Clear your mind and start the morning again. That's it. Go walk outside. Get some lunch—something healthy —a salad, maybe. No coffee this afternoon. Water. Or maybe juice. Yes, that's it. Exercise, healthy food. That always gets a person feeling better.

He stood up. Boy, it sure would have been nice to get something done first. Maybe he could just write a few lines of the real code. Just fifteen or twenty lines. Then he'd have started, and could go, feeling like he'd done something, and then would have a place to start when he came back.

No, no. Then he would have to waste time when he came back, finding the spot where he left off. He'd have to re-read all the lines. Better just to start fresh.

Feeling a little guilty, he put his hand on the mouse and moved the pointer. He paused. Well, his fellow programmer *did* tell him to go to lunch. That's what he would expect him to do now. People like it when you take their advice. And he was probably right.

He clicked, and the computer began the process of shutting down. A few moments later, the low, quiet hum of the hard drive and the fan were silenced, and the screen went dark.

Oops. No reason to shut down the computer for lunch. He usually only shut down at night. Why did he do that? Now he would have to wait for a restart when he came back.

Oh, well. That only takes a couple of minutes. Big deal. And it would be like a fresh start.

He reached over and turned off the lamp before leaving the cubicle.

SCHADENFREUDE

She whipped open the café door and scooted inside out of the cold and wind. A frustrated sigh escaped her lips when she saw four people in line. The tables in the café were about half occupied. As she stood in line, she slowly gazed around the room. At one table, two young women, fairly well-dressed, were looking at the screen of a laptop, reading and discussing something. One of them would occasionally type a few words. She could hear snatches of their conversation: "…then I think we could say…" "…not in the original assessment…" "…uh…let's see…didn't Stacy…." Farther away, two older, graying men in t-shirts sat drinking coffee and talking. She couldn't hear them, but they did not seem too intent on anything in particular. Another table held four teenaged boys drinking cold whipped drinks and talking. Occasionally, they would burst out laughing. Another table, across the room, held three girls, also teenagers. They seemed intent on their own discussion, punctuated by occasional giggles and mock shocked expressions at each other.

School is out, she thought. *That's why there are so many teens here.* Over there, in the corner, a lone man, in a white sweatshirt with large letters reading "Oxford University," was typing madly away on a laptop, oblivious to all. A middle-aged woman sat with a frail elderly woman, drinking tea in silence.

"Hey, Kimmie!" she heard from behind her. She turned around and saw a parent from their children's school, two young children with her: a toddler and a baby in her arms.

"Hi!" she answered. *Darn. What is her name? I see her more than once a week, but we rarely talk. I am so bad with names.*

"What are you doing?" asked the woman without a name, with that irritating upward lilt of tone and a flip of her colored fake hair.

"Oh, I was on my way back home from shopping and just stopped to get a gift card for a Christmas."

"Oh, I should do that. I still have so many gifts to buy. I just picked the kids up from school and—" Her attention suddenly shifted to the right. "*Jason!* Watch what you are doing!"

The toddler had wandered over to a large stand-alone display stacked with individual bags of coffee beans. Reaching for a brightly colored one on the top, the toddler was balancing on his tiptoes. He grabbed the bag and brought it down to his face. "Jason!" The mom shifted her baby to one side.

"I'll get him. You hang on to the baby." She walked the few steps over to the toddler and said, "Hey, uh…" *I can't remember his name either,* "….cutie, come over here and let me see you." The toddler did not respond but kept reaching and grabbed another bag with his chubby hand. Reaching him, she grabbed him under the arms and swung him up onto her hip. "Gotcha!"

He began to cry and mumble something incoherent, struggling to get away. She turned toward the child's mother.

"Thanks…he gets into everything!"

Feeling a bit embarrassed, she walked over and set the child down beside the mom.

The mom looked at the crying boy, holding his upper arm. "Now, Jason, you know better…."

Jason twisted away and turned straight back to the display. His mom reached out and nabbed him. "Now, Jason, you listen to me!" She flipped him around to face her, still balancing the baby.

I hate this. Sure glad my kids aren't like this. She gently pried the coffee bean bag from the toddler as the mom attempted to reason with the little creature. Walking to the display, she set it back in place, feeling a bit awkward: not remembering names, not wanting to discipline another woman's—

As she pulled her hand away from the bag of beans and turned, she immediately realized it was falling. Instinctively grabbing for it, she moved too quickly and knocked the bag into the other neatly stacked rows. A domino effect ensued, worsened by her spastic attempts to try to stop the cascade. The entire row of bags toppled and fell to the floor amidst her floundering. It all happened so quickly. There was silence. She felt everyone in the place looking at her. *Oh. What an idiot!* She hated attention, even when it was good. Now she was just a klutzy woman in the café for everyone to laugh at.

✦

The three teen girls turned to look at the commotion, then back to each other and began giggling, bending over the table to hide their amusement.

"That's funny," the dark-haired one said . "How embarrassing. I am glad it wasn't me."

The long-haired blonde said, "Well, if she didn't have such a big butt, maybe she wouldn't knock into everything," which started a whole new round of giggles.

"You're one to talk," the third girl said with an impish smile. The blonde's eyes flew open in mock horror.

"At least I'm not a slut!"

They all laughed, and the dark-haired one said, "Ooooh. She got you!" Her cell phone began playing a tinny tune. She picked it up and flipped it open.

"Hi, Mom…Yeah, Starbucks…yeah…ok…I'll be there soon." She closed it. "I gotta go." She said her goodbyes, picked up her backpack, and left the café.

It was cold outside. She pulled her jacket close around her, flipped the hood over her head, flung a scarf around her neck, and tucked her face into it. Walking rapidly down the street, she could hardly see anything through the fabric. But she knew the way to the bus stop by heart.

The sounds and sights around her were familiar. A few people passed by: some alone, their thick coats swishing as they hustled in the winter air. The dress shoes of businessmen tapped a rhythm on the sidewalk. Occasionally, a child singing or talking or whining. The *whoosh* of the cars and trucks passing by punctuated the symphony of the city.

She heard a yell. Looking up, a bicycle was coming at her. She instinctively ducked to the side as the rider simultaneously swerved, but the people all around made it a tight move. She found herself on the ground, stunned.

"Are you okay?" said a voice. Blinking her eyes, she looked up at an elderly man, wearing an English-type riding cap. "Uh…yeah," she said, struggling to get up. The backpack and thick clothing made it awkward. She felt the man's hand on her arm, helping her up. "Are you okay?" he repeated.

"Yes. I…." She was confused and embarrassed.

"I *saw* what happened," he said. "That kid wasn't even watching where he was going! And you weren't either. You kids need to pay more attention! Lucky it was you and not an old person. Hips break easily!"

"Sorry." She looked around, noting that several people were watching, some beginning to walk away.

"Alright, well, if you are okay…." The man shuffled off. She looked around to see if she had dropped anything. A little boy was standing on the sidewalk not too far away, waiting with his mother to cross the street. He was staring at her without expression. She took a breath and turned the other way and resumed walking. Her shoulder really hurt. The coat probably prevented any cuts or scrapes, but she was sure she'd have bruises. Maybe a cracked bone.

As she walked, she glimpsed a face inside a store window, staring at her with an amused look. A middle-aged woman at a table with a younger man. The man was grinning. When they caught eyes, the woman turned away.

✦

The boy pedaled faster. "What a moron," he said under his breath. He had almost crashed big-time. *Idiot teenaged girls, always walking with their heads down. There are all so arrogant—think they are the center of the world! Serves her right. She certainly looked stupid getting up. The look on her face!* He laughed to himself.

He weaved in and out of the people on the streets. The bike lane was off to the right of the curb. He knew that there were signs that read "No Bikes" and "No Skateboards" in a few places. They had only put the signs up last year. Probably a bunch of old people and teenaged girls had complained. Gotta protect the world from boys on bikes! He didn't care. It was much too fun to weave in and out. Like playing a video game. And he was a great rider: one of the best at the half-pipe course near his house.

He arrived at a cross street, and, seeing that the light was green, shot off the curb, passing to the right of a man who was walking across. He heard the man yell something, but he ignored it. Probably just startled him. Poor baby. People always telling him what he's doing wrong. Just like his sisters. Telling him he was selfish.

He saw that he was almost at Cochran Street. He glanced across the corner to see if the light was red yet. One of his weekly games on this long ride home was "beat the light." He would adjust his speed and wait for it to turn yellow while he was still a way from the corner. He then sped up, counting to himself (the crossing light lasted thirty seconds, but he had a few seconds more before the cars would actually cross the street). He loved this little game. Every so often he was too far away to make it, and he had to slam on the brakes, skidding the bike sideways up to the corner curb. Usually, if he timed it right, he could make it: he would cut the corner and jump the bike off the sidewalk, swerve into the crosswalk, and it was full speed to the other side, typically before the light even changed red. He especially enjoyed it when the light changed red as he reached the midway point of the crosswalk. This still gave him plenty of time to get to the other side, but it made him feel like a daredevil. He especially loved hearing someone on the sidewalk gasp. He was smarter than all these idiots standing around like mindless cows, waiting for a bell to ring.

The light had turned green not too long ago. Plenty of time. Not much fun today, unless he slowed down considerably. He decided not to: he shot off the sidewalk into the street about fifteen feet from the corner and the crosswalk. As he reached the crosswalk, he leaned sideways and turned towards the far side. A motion to his right startled him. Too late, he spotted a car coming towards him far too fast. He just had time to wonder if the light had already changed or the driver was running the red light.

He felt nothing on impact. He heard screeching tires, crashing, and other chaotic noises. Yelling. Darkness. He became aware of people standing around him. He struggled to get up, and felt tremendous pain on his left side. He fell back, and then someone's hands were on him. The noise began to clear. The pain got worse and he moaned. A voice said, "Just lie still. You're going to be okay. Don't move."

He was sitting at the stoplight in his car, waiting for the light to change. It had seemed to last longer than usual, but he was in no hurry. He enjoyed watching the people cross in front of him. *Look at that guy, in the expensive-looking suit, with the leather briefcase and an earpiece in his ear. He was talking to someone out there. It was probably all an act. He was most likely a nobody, a regular employee, but walking around like that made him feel important.*

A woman crossed the street, ambling slowly. *Wow, she is huge.* Goodness, how does anyone get that large? The tent she wore for a dress flapped in the wind. A kid ran behind her, about five years old. The stereotype of a little urchin, with dirt or candy (or both) smeared on his face. *People. Good thing I don't live like they do.*

He continued his classification of the human race as he watched the pedestrians cross. *Bum. Smart-aleck teen. Stuck-up young businesswoman. Poor, harried soccer mom, so totally caught up in her kids that nothing else exists.*

He saw a motion to the right. A kid on a bike shot out right in front of a quickly moving car. He knew they'd collide. He watched, as if viewing a film in a theater. It seemed to happen in slow motion: the driver slamming on his brakes, the kid looking back at the car at the last moment in surprise, the impact, the body and the bike rocketing up and forward, a twisting mass of wheels, limbs, handlebars. Then the boy and the bike were on the ground. He looked as if he had not hit his head, but one arm was bent in an awkward manner, and his legs were caught up in the bike.

Wow. Hate to be that driver. They'll get him, even though it was the kid's fault. Idiotic. You just can't take chances anymore. People will blame you for anything, even things that are someone else's fault. And they'll have plenty of people chiming in. A society of whiners. A society of victims. And that driver will pay the price. Sure glad I am not him.

The light changed. Several people had gathered around the boy. Three were on cell phones. Help would come fast. He put his car in gear and drove on, passing the scene. The boy raised his head—even seemed to try to lift himself up. *He'll probably be alright. That should teach him a lesson— but probably not.*

He sped up. The next light was farther than the last. Not much traffic for this time of day. There was a woman on the sidewalk with a trendy hairstyle, sun-glasses, and fancy clothes, struggling to carry five or six bags. He caught the name on one: a high-priced international boutique. Of course. More money that she knew what to do with. She wanted to be so *haute couture*: did she know that she looked no different from a bag lady down the street, just pricier? *Glad I am just a normal guy, normal life, normal desires.*

To his right, up ahead, he glimpsed two women and a child exiting a café in a bustle. One woman held a baby in one hand and a bag in the other. The second woman had a coffee cup in one hand, and with the other was trying to control the toddler. He kept twisting away from her. As he approached, the toddler suddenly made a dash for the street, right in front of his car. His heart jumped, he swerved to the left, keeping his eye on the child, relieved that his swerve was successful. A loud horn sounded, and he looked back to the front. A truck was coming at him. He whipped the wheel to the right on instinct, knowing it was too late. The truck, also swerving, caught his car along its side. The world spun. He was in the midst of a flying glass and metal tornado. He caught a glimpse out the window, like a brief photograph, of the two women, the baby, the child, and the coffee cup, frozen in time, watching him expressionlessly.

So glad I'm not them, he thought.

NON FUI, FUI, NON SUM, NON CURO

I am lost at sea, washed overboard during a terrific storm which nearly capsized the boat several times. It is dark.

I have not caught a glimpse of the ship in some time. How long has it been? Hours? Days? Time has no meaning out here. Is this what eternity feels like to a deity? It is like a dream, though the pain and fear and exhaustion remind me that it is quite real.

Did I have another life before this? *That* seems like a dream more than this.

Swells are sixty feet high, cresting and crashing at the top. The water is biting cold. I fight constantly to keep my head above water, but every time a swell lifts me up, I am tossed into the air at the crest, a free-fall that seems to last forever, my heart catching in my throat, waiting for that sudden plunge back into the churning water. I almost suffocate until I can orient myself and fight back to the surface, gulping great gasps of air and spray, which cause me to choke.

Beyond tired. Exhaustion. Maybe a stronger person could keep it up until they are rescued. If rescue comes. Somewhere in my mind I know that floating on my back and resting is what I *need* to do, but in such swells and storms and rain, I just don't have the strength. If I was in better shape, if I was stronger, perhaps I could. But I am tossed about like a little stuffed animal in a dryer. Like a leaf tumbling down a wintry street.

At first, I tried making my shirt into a flotation device, just as we were taught in safety classes. But I cannot get it sealed, and the air won't hold. I tried rolling myself into a ball to hold still and relax, go with the swells, stretching out and breathing at intervals, but the tossing and turning and spinning makes it impossible.

I tried dropping underwater after a deep breath, relaxing until the air is gone, then back up, hoping for respite beneath the washing machine-like churning. But in such a storm, any calm waters must be far below. The cold saps my strength, and my ability to hold my breath becomes shorter and shorter. All the tricks I know. All of my training. Useless.

I tried pushing upwards at the top of the waves to look for a ship, lights, or land. My physical strength is waning. The cold, the exertion, the swallowing of water, the gasping for air. I panic when I am forced below the surface, and, as the violent sea spins and flips me, I cannot tell which way is up.

Just as all seems lost, and I will drown, I become oriented and kick to the surface. My leg muscles ache, my whole body aches, and my lungs have water in them. If the ship is still out there, maybe they will rescue me. I have prayed and prayed for deliverance, for the storm to stop. Land might be nearby, but I would not see it. Ships and helicopters would not dare come out into this maelstrom.

God does not answer.

Humans do not answer.

Do I keep fighting until the last of my strength is gone? Or just give up now, let all the air out, and sink? The latter goes against human nature—survival is our innate drive. I would prefer it be *my* choice when I die. Maybe if I swam far enough down, I would not make it up in time before I blacked out. It would be over.

I wish the fight for survival would leave me. It is hopeless.

Of course, at some point I won't have the strength left, and then it won't matter any longer. There will be no decisions to make.

Occasionally, I imagine I hear a sound. Is it a boat? Is it a horn? Is it my ship calling for me? Or is it tricks of a mind pushed beyond its limits? I see lights, too. Lightning? My ship's searchlight? Or just tricks of the optical nerve, straining in the watery darkness?

I hear a voice say, *Come on! Don't give up. If you give up, you'll die. It is up to you to hang on.*

I hate that voice. But it goes on.

Come on. Suck it up, sailor. People have been through worse. You can't choose your circumstances, but you can choose how you react to them.

Wise sayings can't save anyone.

What can I do? Up and down, tossed about. Submerged, lost underwater, gasping for air, down again. Incredible fatigue like I have never known. Sleep, food, air, warmth…faint memories that I can no longer grasp. If only I was more courageous. More disciplined. More stoic.

Perhaps what matters at this moment is *how* I face death. There can be meaning in one's demise. Facing it with calm resolve and resignation. Maybe now is my time to show my mettle. Accept the end with nobility. The ancient Romans understood this. Everyone's time comes. It is no big deal. The famous inscription found on so many Roman graves sums it up: *Non fui, fui, non sum, non curo.* "I was not, I was, I am not, I care not." What is the difference if I live or die? People come, people go. The world goes on.

It's all up to you. If you only had the right attitude, and faced your fears and suffering properly, then everything would be well.

Tepid platitudes from those who stand outside the storm, where everything is clear and clinical.

I'm thinking the Romans were right.

LOUISON

P risoner! To the far wall!"
He knew this routine. It was the same every time they brought the bucket. But it had only been one day. Did he miscount? Were they altering the routine to throw him off?

He rose slowly and hobbled to the far wall and stood facing the door, as required. The door opened the rest of the way, and he saw his guard, but no bucket. Instead, standing beside the guard was another man. His livery and the gilded sword betrayed that he was an officer of some importance, not a common jailer. As if to punctuate that fact, the man's face cringed at the stench. "*Merde!*" he said with a turn of his head. He recovered quickly: a trained soldier.

"Nicolas Pelletier," spoke the officer. "I am Antoine Brissot, the official representative of Charles-Henri Sanson, the High Executioner of France. I am here to inform you of your sentence," he said, in a formal voice with his chin slightly raised. "For the crimes of highway thievery, tomorrow morning at 9 o'clock you will be put to death."

Nicolas was not surprised, but it was still stunning to hear the words spoken. The room spun, his vision dimmed, he felt numb. He had known this would be his fate soon after his arrest and brief trial. Highway robbery was a serious crime in France, more so than common thievery, for it preyed on the wealthy as they travelled in their fancy stagecoaches. Still, it was impossible for a human not to hold out for some hope for reprieve, or mercy, or *something*. The sure knowledge of one's death, even if expected, is more than the mind can fully conceive. This life—his existence—was his only frame of reference. He had seen death, he had known people who existed and then did not. He had sometimes been the cause of their demise. But he could not fathom his own nonexistence. He wondered if he should be more upset. Should he scream? Sob? Beg? None of those emotions came. He just stood.

"I am also to inform you," Brissot continued, and Nicolas noticed that a bit of sardonic glee had crept into his tone. Others may not have noticed this shift, but an imprisoned man begins to notice more details than the free man, for his world has become minuscule, and small islands transform themselves into vast continents. "I am also to inform you that the *Assemblée nationale* has recently decided that the purpose of the death penalty is not to make a sinner suffer, but to remove him from society. Therefore, you will not be hanged, beheaded, or dismembered. Instead, you will be put to death humanely and quickly with a new French invention."

This piqued the interest of Nicolas in a strange, detached way. Almost as if he were researching and writing a document on the death of some other criminal. He found himself interested in his own interest.

"You will be the first to be executed employing this new device. It is called the *louison*. The Parisian crowds are ecstatic to see this new device used. So your infamy continues, right up to the moment of your death!"

He paused, obviously for dramatic effect, which seemed childish to Nicolas, considering the present audience. "In fact, I believe this new device was invented by an Alsacian. You hail from Strasbourg, is it not so?"

Nicolas nodded.

"I thought so. A certain Monsieur Laquiante is the inventor. You might know him, since he is an officer of the *court* in Strasbourg." He smiled at his clever remark.

"No," Nicolas replied with more bravado than he felt, "most of my work was around Île-de-France." It felt good to be flippant at this moment, though he did not know why.

The liveried officer looked at him a moment, as if considering whether Nicolas' response was sarcasm or just a statement of the truth. The officer waved dismissively. "Eh, bien." He nodded to the guard, and with a flourish and a slam of the door, they were gone.

The cell was dark and damp. The dirt floor was covered with dried rushes. Dirty. Decomposing. There was no bench, no chair, no low stone bed. The prisoner sat huddled in one corner, where he had collected together some rushes to make a faux cushion to sit upon. It made the floor a bit warmer, but the cold emanating from the nearby walls seeped through his thin garment like rain-soaked freshly dug turf. At least it was warmer now that it was April—much better than the winter, when it gets so cold in the center of Paris.

His excrement was piled in the far corner of the cell, a largely psychological attempt to remove himself from the stench and possible diseases he might contract. The guards tossed an empty bucket into his cell every few days, for him to collect his defecation with his hands and fill the bucket, which they then removed. He was unable to wash his hands (or any other part of him), except when they delivered his food once a day. This invariably consisted of a hunk of cheese, a thick slice of bread, and a bowl of water on a board. Since he also needed the water to drink, he avoided washing his hands until he had finished eating. This required eating with one hand—the hand he didn't use for his toilet—and saving enough water to wash himself. These meager attempts at hygiene and health had little effect on the piss-and-shit smell of the cell, or on his health. He felt constantly filthy, but the ritual made him feel like he had some control over his miserable life.

The heavy wooden door to the cell, reinforced with iron, had a small opening three-quarters of the way up —just large enough for a guard to look in and check on him, or to pass the board through. There was no window, but a faint, indirect light came through the window in the door from the torches that lined the walls of the prison. He had only seen that hallway once, seven weeks ago, when he had been brought here. He was pretty sure it had been seven weeks. Each time he was fed, he had been making little scratches on the floor in the third corner. He assumed they corresponded to days, though he did not have cycles of light and dark known for sure.

To an outside observer, it would appear that he was simply curled up in the corner, hugging his knees, staring out into the cell, unmoving. Every few moments, his head moved slightly. This outside observer might assume that he had lost his mind or was in such a stupor from the beatings and the conditions. Maybe he was reflecting on his crimes. Perhaps he was wondering what would happen to him.

In reality, he was engaged in a mental exercise. The cell was made of stones, cut into roughly rectangular shapes. The stones appeared to be a dirty white-gray color, but without more light he could not be sure. The first row of blocks were laid end to end, and he could see the mortar that had been slopped between them when the prison was built. Some of it was crumbling, but the stones were so close together, and so large, that his investigations had revealed that there was no chance of digging one out. Besides, what he knew of the prison told him that even if he did, there would be so many more obstacles beyond this cell that it would be a futile effort anyway.

The next row of blocks was laid on top of the others, but staggered so that each block was sitting half on one below, half on the next. The result was that no mortar line ran straight up the wall, a standard building device to add stability. The third row was back in line with the first row, and this alternating pattern continued to the ceiling, which was made of thick wood beams, topped by more stones, and, he assumed, another cell above that.

His mental exercise consisted of counting the blocks. He began at the top wall opposite the door and counted across. On the alternating rows, where the builders began with a half-block, he counted one half. Once finished with one wall, he began on the wall to its left, then on the wall to its right. To count the blocks of the wall in which the door was set, he had to crawl to the center of the cell and look back at it. He used to stand and count, but he was so weak these days that he simply sat. He wasn't sure if he was sick or if the paucity of diet was affecting him. He had performed this exercise many times. Occasionally, he lost count when his mind wandered. When this happened, he forced himself to start over each time until he finished counting the entire room. Sometimes he came up with different numbers, slightly off by one or two from a previous counting. Then he knew he had made a mistake. Usually, the number came to 321 and a half, so he was pretty sure this was the correct number. It was a mind-numbing exercise that took him out of his environment, out of his condition, and into a world dominated by the order of exact counting.

Once finished, he would try to sleep. If he could, he began the exercise again, until his mind was so weary that he slumbered.

✦

The cell was dark and damp. The prisoner was curled up in one of the corners, staring out at the opposite wall. He was in the midst of his mental exercise when a noise at the door startled him to reality. Keys jangled at the door. The door swung open and slammed against the back wall. The prisoner jumped. In came Brissot and two soldiers.

"Prisoner! On your feet!"

He blinked. Something was different.

As he struggled to his feet, hand on one wall to steady himself, he realized that he had not been told to go to the far wall. As he stiffly came upright, one soldier went across the cell to stand behind him, while the other strode a bit further into the middle of the cell. As he moved, the prisoner saw two or three other soldiers standing at attention outside the cell. The prisoner realized their muskets were in the ready position.

So this was it.

"Follow me!" Brissot shouted, unnecessarily loud, it seemed to Nicolas. Brissot turned. As Nicolas followed him, the two soldiers fell in behind. The rest of the soldiers—maybe four or five of them—took places in front and behind. As they marched, his mind raced. Moments of sheer panic, interspersed with analysis and thoughts that seemed such a contrast to the doom that lay ahead. As they moved through the darkened corridor, Nicolas became aware of other doors along both sides. Part of his mind wondered about the prisoners in those cells. What fate were they awaiting? He knew that this prison, the Prison de la Grand Roquette, housed both those to be executed and those awaiting less harsh punishments.

What was this new device, this *louison*? Nicolas did not really fear death, though he used to. When he spurred his horse and descended upon an unsuspecting carriage, he always experienced fear and anxiety. What if the coach driver had a musket and Nicolas could not get to him before he could shoot? What if one of the passengers was a soldier? All unlikely. Still, he worried. Sometimes, when he have visited Paris, cloaked and hooded, he feared that he would be recognized, and the authorities would descend upon him. But he had feared these things anyway, and he had feared death. No longer. The time in prison, waiting for his execution, had cured him of that particular fear. Now, he feared pain and suffering. He had seen men tortured to death—even a couple of his own acquaintances. Dismemberment was common. The prisoner howled like a tortured animal as the executioner held his unattached limbs before his face. Disembowelment—the prisoner watching the hooded butcher pull out bloody entrails—the parts of one's body that are never supposed to see the light of day. The indescribable smell which could sicken the hardiest of the hardy. Then the unfortunate man was hanged, and the strangled cries and strange contortions continued until the body finally hung still. All the while, the crowd yelling and screaming and cheering—a modern equivalent to the Roman gladiator shows.

But this new thing, this *louison*—what did this word mean? What torture would he endure?

The hallway curved. He had obviously seen it before, but he did not remember. Soon they came to another hallway, crosswise to the current one, but not exactly at a ninety-degree angle. It was larger, and well-lit. He blinked, for his eyes had not seen this much light in some time. Again, part of his mind wondered how bright it would seem to a normal person. Far down the hall was a brighter light, up high. A window?

What if Bissot was playing with him? An innovation for punishing the worst of criminals? Nicolas had heard nothing of this. But he knew how executions worked. The people gathered to see the suffering, to cheer someone else's pain. "There but for the grace of God…" Or rather, "There is a person far worse than me…" We hate most what we fear in ourselves. "Am I capable of doing what he did?" The thought terrifies us, so we must kill it, wipe it out, so it can no longer re-mind us of our own flaws. Much safer than trying to understand it.

His company slowed and then stopped near the win-dow or opening, now high above. Nicolas' eyes contin-ued to adjust. He saw two massive wooden doors in front of him, crossed and beamed with iron. He could hear a faint buzzing sound coming from somewhere.

A few words were exchanged between Bissot and a guard, then the clanking of heavy chains and locks echoed back down the stone corridors. Dimly, he saw two of the soldiers busy at the doors, struggling with weighty chains and bolts. Soon the noise stopped, and each guard grabbed one large door handle. Leaning forward and pushing with all their weight, they began to push open the doors.

A sliver of illumination appeared, running vertically from the floor to high above his head—almost to the initial light above. The sliver grew wider, and the light grew brighter, as if a rip in the universe was opening to disclose the very throne room of God. Nicolas realized that the buzzing he heard was the noise of a large crowd talking and murmuring beyond the doors.

Soon the light was so intense that it hurt. The guards began to move forward, but he could hardly make out anything in the bright light. A shove from behind made him stumble to his knees, as if he was falling in mercy before the *Shekinah*. He blinked and squinted.

"On your feet, prisoner!" someone nearby shouted, and he was grabbed by both arms and hoisted to his feet. For a moment, the aroma of soap touched his nostrils—bodies nearby that had recently washed themselves with clean water. How long had it been since he felt that? This was the closest to a human he had been in some time. Since he had been thrown into his cell, no one had touched him. He felt a sensation of intimacy—strange since these were guards who cared not a whit for him, who were leading him to his death. Yet, it seemed that even the touch of a human who intends to kill you is better than no touch at all.

On his feet and moving forward slowly now, without the help of the guards, he moved through the large doorway. The overwhelming light began to fade and resolve into details. He could now see that the day was not sunny or bright at all, but overcast. The public square before him was moving and undulating with a mass of people. The close-packed buildings of various sizes and ages lined the square, with streets running off in different directions, leading out to the rest of the city. Something large stood directly between him and the crowd. A fountain? A statue?

He was led directly towards the object, and as he drew near, he saw that the monument was not a monument at all, but a tall, wooden frame of some sort. It sat on a plinth of stone.

"Step," said a quiet voice to his right. He looked down, and noticed the cobbled street and, just ahead, a short flight of stairs, barely wide enough for three to walk abreast. He climbed the steps and was brought to stand before the massive frame, towering at least three times as high as a man. Two hooded men stood beside the structure.

Nicolas looked in confusion at the bottom of the frame. There was a thick board, set on its edge, running from one side to the other; the top about two feet off the ground. At the middle was a shallow, half-circle cutout. Nicolas immediately thought of "stocks," and the presence of metal brackets on either side of the vertical struts confirmed it. A second board, leaning against the side of the structure, with a similar half-circle cut, matched up to the bottom board. The prisoner placed his neck on the half-circle, the guards slid the other board on top and locked it in place. The prisoner was fixed with his head caught between the two boards.

What was this? Stocks were used for punishment as a public humiliation, not for executions. The criminal was on public display, like a trapped animal, where the righteous masses could ridicule the ugly beast, spit upon him, and use his head for target practice with rotten fruit and garbage.

Were they going to lock him in there and *then* dismember him? Swing the axe at his head? That would seem to make the chance of missing a clean cut through the neck more likely. Yet there was not a chopping block underneath where his head would be. And what would be "merciful" about all that?

He raised his eyes, looking up at the tall structure. Why so tall?

Then he saw it. Understanding dawned upon him. At the top of the structure, suspended by a rope between the two struts, was a large, heavy iron blade. Its bottom was finely honed to a sharp edge. It curved down in the middle and back up on the sides by the struts. The rope which suspended the blade went through a series of pulleys, then off to the side, then slanting down to the edge of the platform. There, it was tied securely to a metal cleat, like a boat of death moored to a dock. Next to the cleat stood an oaf of a man, dressed in black with a hood over his eyes with only his mouth and chin visible, prepared to cast off this grisly vessel on its maiden voyage.

The crowd roared. Nicolas became aware that Bissot had been standing at the front of the platform, speaking to them. He looked out over the people, a blur of humans packed together in every space: in front of the platform and on the sides, spreading out like a strange carpet of hair, hats, hoods, and bonnets, filling the space all the way to the buildings and down the adjoining streets as far as he could see. More people lived in the Eleventh Arrondissement than any other section in Paris —the most densely populated area in any city in Europe—and it appeared they had all turned out to watch Nicolas and his appointment with the *louison*.

Nicolas was terrified. What was this? Was the blade lowered slowly? Quickly? Did it take a slice through the neck a bit at a time, lowering and raising repeatedly, until enough blood was spilled, or until the spine was severed? Did they drop it, only to stop inches above the neck, inflicting terror on the poor bastard, over and over again?

He realized that Bissot had stopped speaking, and the crowd was yelling again. Hands grabbed his arms again from either side to force him forward. This time, Nicolas felt no intimacy. Panic began to rise.

"To your knees," said the voice at his side. He was pushed down to kneel before the device. He began to struggle, though he knew it was no use. Fear and panic were his masters now, despite his previous resolve to meet his death with studied stoicism. He had played the scene in his mind often while in his cell. He intended that his last act of defiance would be to rob the bastards of any pleasure in his death. But he thought he knew his fate. Hanging, disembowelment—such horrible torture—but he *knew* them for what they were. He had seen it many times. This unknown device, his unknown fate—he had no preparation.

The foreman forced his head down and his neck into the shallow cut. They held him down, struggling, as the top board was placed on top. He fought with himself not to cry out, but the pounding and screaming inside his head was deafening as the board was latched into place. The crowd yelled and shouted. Suddenly he was released. He pulled and pushed against the boards. He felt himself going mad. A moan and a whimper escaped his mouth. He fought not to cry out.

The crowd full silent, as if the whole mob caught its breath at once. He stopped struggling for a moment, a moment in which he thought maybe he could accept this unknown fate. Then, like an avalanche, an overwhelming panic took over as this novel horror awaited him. His struggles grew frantic.

"*Commencez!*" a voice shouted. The hollering of the crowd grew louder. A cry erupted unbidden from his throat. A deep, moaning, animal-like plea of fear. He defecated. The crowd noise swelled. Above him, there was a wooden and metallic clunk. Like a stagecoach being unhitched from its horses.

Metal scraped on wood.

BATTLE-WEARY

Cool air touched his bare shoulder and startled him awake. He opened his eyes.

"It is daybreak, my lord." Merlyn stood in the tent door, his left hand holding open the flap. Arthur blinked, trying to focus his sleepy eyes. His old friend and mentor was looking at him without expression, though somewhere deep in those gray eyes, Arthur could see compassion and love. The long grey beard covered much of his face, but weariness and fatigue were apparent.

Arthur took a deep breath. "Have you even slept, my friend?"

Merlyn shrugged. "A bit. Sleep is a luxury I cannot easily afford." Arthur knew where Merlyn had been all night: up at the top of Tor Pen, praying and interceding for Arthur and the soldiers. As he had done every night since before the battle had begun.

"I suppose. You know best. And we need your power."

Merlyn looked up at the far corner of the royal tent and squinted one eye. "I fear my power and your strength may not be enough this time, Arthur. The Saxon evil is strong."

"Aye, it is. And my men are all weary or dying—or dead. But the Lord is with us, no? Am I not his anointed? Are you not his prophet? Do we not have a mission for all of Britannia?"

"I have known this to be so since you were a boy and before. But that does not mean that God's plan does not change: it takes other paths, other roads, unforeseen passes and fords. God's plans are not about the people who are his hands, but about the road he is laying. He uses and discards as suits his purpose."

"Yes, yes, I know, my dour friend. I have heard you say it many times. 'And we are but servants to serve as He wills; mere building blocks for his masterful plan.'"

The druid smiled and nodded. "Indeed." He turned and looked over his shoulder, holding the tent flap open a bit more. Arthur could see the cold, clear dawn. The twenty-third day of the battle, here in Chichester. He felt another brush of cold air. He pulled the layers of animal skins up to his neck and felt a tremendous soreness in his arm muscles. He grunted in pain.

Merlyn turned back into the tent. "The cooks have finished preparing breakfast. I will have Powys bring you some."

"Thank you, Merlyn."

The old druid stood looking at the king, unmoving. Arthur could not read the look in his eyes. Arthur started to speak, but Merlyn quickly turned and left. The heavy fabric of the tent flap swept closed, and the room was plunged into gloom.

Arthur took a deep breath. This movement revealed more soreness in his stomach and chest muscles. He groaned. Steeling himself, he flung the coverings aside and swung his feet around to sit up at the side of the bed. The pain caused him to catch his breath. There did not seem to be one place on his body that did not ache. His upper left arm throbbed where the medic had cleaned and bandaged the wound he had received from a deflected Saxon spear. It had flown in from the side, having glanced off another man's shield. A chance flip caused it to careen in behind Arthur's shield. Though the spear's velocity was abated, the steel blade was sharp and heavy enough to cut through his leather sleeve and cause a shallow wound that, nevertheless, bled profusely.

He bent over slightly and looked at his left thigh, just below his hip. A week-old wound was healing, though each day's fighting hindered the healing process. A Saxon, whose sword arm Arthur had just removed from his body, lunged up with his dirk in the only hand he had left, catching Arthur on his thigh. It was not deep, for the man did not have the strength to make a full lunge, and Arthur was able to leap back. The man fell at his feet, and Arthur swung Excalibur down upon the man's back with full force, ending the man's suicide attempt to wound or kill Arthur and thus demoralize the Britons. Yet Arthur was wounded, and he had to call his guards around him to withdraw. Powys staunched the wound and bound it quickly, before Arthur waded back into the melee to rally his men—for the fourth time that day.

He lifted his eyes from his reverie and looked across the tent. In the dim light he could see the small wooden table upon which the faint outlines of a pile of clothes and armor lay. His massive sword leaned against the side of the table. A familiar stench came to his nostrils: a combination of sweat, leather, metal, and old blood. Blood, once alive and flowing, now soaked and dried into cloth and leather, caked in the crevices and ruts of the metal in places where no amount of cleaning and packing with herbs could remove. A sickening smell, for not only was it a reminder of the graphic and bloody nature of life these days, but a reminder of the *feeling* of battle itself. The fog, the confusion, the sounds: screams, groans, grunts, metal clanging. Rarely time to think, only time to react. Running, turning, slashing, thrusting; arms, legs, eyes, mouth; fear, relief, pain, defiance.

Despite the sleep, he was exhausted. His body ached. His mind ached. The thought of putting on his armor once more was almost unbearable. The thought of fighting again, more so. Let it all end. Give in to the Saxons. Let them have their victory. Would it be so bad? They would certainly kill him. Publicly, after torture and humiliation. Still, death would come eventually, and it would be a relief.

Arthur took a deep breath and let out a long, slow sigh. It would be easier. But giving up was not an option. There were friends to save, there were lands to defend, there were innocent people to protect. The cost was high, but worth fighting for. Worth being wounded for. Worth dying for. *I must remember that, and keep myself from focusing on the moments of pain and weariness, or surely I shall not make it*.

The tent flap swung aside and Powys strode in.

"Greetings, my lord," he said without cheer. "It is a fine morning: clear and still. A good day for battle. Remember, my king, when you go into battle, you fight two enemies: the one in front of you, and the one inside you." He headed over to the brazier.

Arthur grunted. "Must you say that every morning, Powys?"

Powys stopped and frowned. "You requested that I speak those words each morning of battle."

The king smiled. "Yes, I know." Powys was sometimes too serious.

Powys picked up a poker and stirred the embers. He added some kindling stacked beside the brazier and spread them among the half-burned wood and ashes. A candle from a metal stand nearby served to relight the fire. He then lit the other five candles which were in the stand. The room's dimness diminished as he lit each, revealing a sparsely furnished tent. A rough-hewn bed, a table, and a chair, the brazier, two large iron candle stands, and two short stools. Near the bed, by the tent wall, was a large clay pot. A towel hung above it on a peg. On the table, next to the pile of clothes and armor, lay some parchments, a writing stylus, and a half-empty bottle of ink. A plain wooden cross, about a foot tall, stood in an empty corner of the tent.

The room was bright now. "Someone will be along shortly with hot water, food, and drink, my king. The men are preparing and will be ready for assembly at sunrise. How are your wounds?"

"Fine. Troublesome, but no worse."

"I'll send the medic to check them and dress them."

"No need. Go get yourself some food and take some time for yourself to prepare."

"Already done, my lord. Do you require anything else?"

Arthur looked bemusedly at Powys. He suspected that he had gotten up hours earlier, washed, eaten, taken care of the men, waited on his king, and was prepared to do more work. Yet he seemed to take it all very matter-of-factly. He took care of himself, took care of Arthur, and took care of others, got less sleep than most, and yet fought in the same battle as the rest, for the same number of days.

Arthur looked up and squinted at Powys. "Yes, there is one more thing. Take my place as leader of the troops. I think you are made of much sterner stuff than I."

Powys raised his eyebrows in surprise. "Not even close, my lord! You are chosen for this moment. You are king of the Britons. There is none like you."

Arthur looked down at the ground, suddenly sober. "Aye, it would seem so. For good or for ill. But it often feels like just an accident. How I got here, I don't know. And how I will get through it, I don't know."

Powys considered for a moment, then softened his usually formal demeanor. Arthur saw his old friend, not a king's servant. They had known each other since they were young boys. "We all think that, at times, Arthur. How did I get here? Who do I think I am?"

"Even you, my steady friend?"

Powys blinked. "Of course. Some of us just keep working and keep busy so we don't have to reflect. I work hard because I am scared of what thoughts I might have should I pause. But you and Merlyn: you reflect. You agonize. You question yourselves. It is your great strength, but also your great burden. And we are all thankful you do that work so we do not have to."

Arthur pursed his lips. Hard times reveal the weaknesses and the fears in us all, but they also reveal true character. A phrase Merlyn repeated almost daily the last few days. *And right now, my character says, "stay in bed, confess sickness or an infected wound. Let Merlyn lead the troops today. One day….just one day of rest. Then I'll go back out. Please, God, just one day. One hour of peace. One hour of painless rest. Please."*

"Do you need anything else, my king?"

"No, Powys, all is well. I will see you at the assembly ground shortly."

Powys nodded with affection and left the tent.

Arthur stood up, every muscle protesting. Walking to the fire, he stood as close as he could without burning himself on the metal. He desired the heat to work its way into his muscles, through the ligaments and tendons, deep into his body, into the bones themselves. Teasingly, the heat only reached his skin. Ah, for the hot springs of Aqua Sulis! To soak in those ancient Celtic baths, the Roman ruins all around…to lie for hours and allow the heat to soak completely through his pummeled and wounded flesh. To loosen the tendons, to warm the organs, to ease the joints. Someday, when this was over—if he lived—he would make the journey there and do just that.

He turned and allowed the heat to warm his back. He stretched his arms up and overhead, feeling the soreness in his sides, arms, and neck. He began his daily routine of stretching and moving, preparing his body for the day ahead. Each morning, the pain and the soreness seemed worse. But once he had stretched, bathed, eaten, and warmed up with the men, he usually felt better. And once on the battlefield, the pain and lack of resolution disappeared—or, more probably, the adrenaline masked the fearsome pain. It is remarkable what the body and mind can withstand. Such punishment, day after day, until all the days run together. One would think the body would rebel at some point, that it would simply shout, "no more!" and refuse to cooperate with the mind any longer. *Maybe it will, eventually*, Arthur thought. *But not this day*.

"Lord Arthur?" came a voice from outside the tent.

"Yes, come," Arthur responded, as he continued to stretch. A young serving-boy entered, struggling to carry a large leather water-bag. He lurched his way over to the clay pot and set the bag down, holding the top upright so it would not fall over. Arthur could smell the boy's sweat: he had been working hard already this morning. The servant untied the top of the bag and, leaning it over the top of the bowl, lifted it from the bottom while supporting the narrow mouth. Steam rose and swirled in the candlelight as he poured the water.

The servant left as Arthur finished his stretching. Bending and squatting were quite difficult. He was like an old man, his body rusted and creaky. Standing, he walked over to the bowl and knelt before it. Dipping his hands into the water, he scooped it upon his face three times. "Thank you, my dear God, for hot water," he whispered quietly after each scoop. Truthfully, it was not very hot. Not like at Caerleon Castle. Ah, to be back there again. Standing on the parapet, looking out over the sea as it pounded the cliffs below. To be in the Great Hall, the massive fires blazing in the fireplaces, the tables loaded with meat, bread, and ale. The laughter, the noise, the music. To be in his bedchamber, to lay on the huge oak bed with Gwenhwyfar. How much she had wanted to accompany him here. She who had often been in battle herself. Celtic women were as tough as Celtic men, learning swordplay and shield-work while young, just as the boys did. Not like the Saxons, or the Angles, or the Norse, whose women did not battle, but remained cowering at home. The enemy was made up of only males, who razed the towns and farms of Britannia and Caledonia, burning and raping and killing, taking the young women and girls with them along their marches, until they tired of them or used them up, leaving their bodies beside the evil swaths they cut across this fair isle. Many had been the occasion that Briton scouts had reported finding the bodies of girls as Arthur's army chased the Saxons. Once, Arthur himself had found a girl, hidden in the woods beside the road.

She was physically and mentally beaten. Dirty, starved, and bloodied. Some Saxon bastard had probably thought her dead and tossed her beside the road. She had crawled up behind a large stone to hide and die. Arthur had heard a moan as he passed by and, climbing from his horse to investigate, discovered her there. She could not, or would not, speak. She stared blankly, refusing to make eye contact. Nor did she resist as Arthur gathered her up in his arms and gave her to Powys to take to the medic wagon.

What type of humans were these Saxons? Arthur had killed many men himself, of course. Rarely had he killed a woman, though, and only then when absolutely necessary to save his own life or the life of someone else. But this wanton and evil use of people, not caring about the damage or the hurt or the consequences. Arthur knew war was a horror. All nations engaged in it. It had always been around, and always would be. But armies that fought one another for land, or to defend themselves, or to right some wrong is quite different from simply choosing a peaceful village at random and destroying it and its inhabitants. Those villages were no danger to the Saxons. Even if the Saxons felt they needed new lands, and wished to live and use the British Isles, it did not excuse their actions towards people who were no threat to them: they had no weapons and no training. But the Saxons had no care for the innocent. Only for their own selfish and immediate needs.

Yet, have I not done the same at times?

He thought back to a raid he led near Caer Colun during an early Saxon landing on the western shores of Britannia. The raid was prompted by a report that the enemy had landed at a small fishing port and were attacking the nearby villages. A messenger had travelled all day to reach Arthur at Londinium. Arthur had quickly assembled a small raiding party and made for Colun. He pushed his men to travel hard all night. It was dangerous to ride horses at a quick pace in the dark, though there had been a half moon after the first hour. The rapid pace enabled Arthur and his men to arrive at the Saxon camp in the dead of night, after the third watch. All the Saxons were asleep after a day of fighting, looting, and raping. Ascertaining the size of the camp and its arrangement, Arthur ordered his men to sweep down upon the camp and kill the defenseless men and burn the camp, making sure there were no escapees and no survivors. He intended the Saxons back home to believe that their fellow men had come to Briton and disappeared without a trace.

As the killing began, however, Arthur heard screams of women, and even a baby crying. Soon Powys found him in the melee, and the two of them retreated quickly to a small shack near the edge of the village on the shore.

"Arthur, there are families here. Women. Children. We don't know who they are, though they are probably Britons. Unless the Saxons brought families this time. Or captives from another landing. Shall I call a retreat?"

Arthur hesitated. He did not have enough men to fight a group this size without the element of surprise. If he stopped the attack, he would have to retreat and return to Londinium to gather a larger army, or withdraw and send for reinforcements. Either way, the Saxons would continue their raids, moving up and down the coast to the next village. He wanted to send for Merlyn, but there was no time. The sounds of battle were all through the beach camp: killing, screaming, running, clashing. He could still hear a woman's voice screaming. The crying baby had stopped.

"Go find Merlyn and bring him here," he said in a low voice.

Powys ran off. Arthur stood staring out the opening of the wood shack at the dark sea, trying to ignore both the sounds and his thoughts. Soon Merlyn arrived and Arthur explained the situation to him. Merlyn, of course, had heard the voices of women and children as well. As Arthur finished telling Merlyn of Powys' report and his thoughts about the options, Powys returned.

"Sir, the camp is just about secured. We caught them completely unawares. A few Saxons at the far end of the camp escaped on foot to the south, but Finn sent five on horseback to track them down. They will catch them. The rest are working their way through the camp to make sure none are left alive. It seems as if we have prevailed."

Merlyn looked at Arthur. "I suppose that makes your decision for you."

Arthur took a long, slow breath. "Aye." He hung his head. "How I despise such killing. Innocents. It should not happen. I should have considered that before we attacked."

"How could you have known, my friend? The Saxon armies do not usually have women at primary camps. Maybe these are village women from yesterday. Or perhaps they brought their own women this time. But they still followed the same tactic of attacking the small villages to kill and rape and loot. You did nothing wrong."

"I am aware of that. I cannot foresee everything, as much as I would like." He took a deep breath again, and looked over at Merlyn, who cocked his head to the side. The fire from a nearby hut lit up the druid's face. "But it makes us like them in a manner of speaking. Killing whoever is in our way in order to accomplish our aims."

"Och, it was an unforeseen incident. You had no way of knowing until it was too late. It is tragic, especially if they *were* our own women or children. But your guilt is unnecessary."

Arthur turned on him. "Guilt?! Who said anything about guilt?!"

Merlyn was taken aback by the sudden vehemence. "Guilt would be understandable, Arthur, even if unmerited. Leaders make bad decisions sometimes. Even the great ones." He paused. "Even the ones appointed by God."

Arthur yelled in anger. "*My* decisions can lead to *death*, and this time to the death of innocents! Maybe I am *not* appointed by God! Perhaps I am here by my own devices and desires!"

Merlyn raised his hand. "Calm down, my king."

"Don't tell me to calm down, old man!" Arthur turned away and strode toward the ocean. "You don't have the responsibility I do!" he shouted over his shoulder.

Powys, having been standing during all of this with his head bowed, looked up at Merlyn. Merlyn was watching Arthur, who, having reached the surf, stood staring out at the sea.

Merlyn turned to Powys. "Choose ten men to set up a brief camp for us at a place they deem best. Put Dawydd in charge. Select four other men to forage for food for breakfast. Have them search the camp first, and if there are no provisions, have them fish or hunt. Have the rest of the men continue the cleanup."

"Aye, my lord."

Merlyn stood for a while after Powys left, looking at the motionless figure of Arthur. Finally, he walked down to the sea to stand beside the king. The smell of the brine, mingled with smoke, was pungent. The air was cool and damp. They stood side-by-side, both staring out to sea.

Merlyn broke the silence. "When you found out there were women and children here, you sent for me."

Arthur cleared his throat. "Yes."

"Why? There were only two options: Continue, or stop and retreat."

Arthur turned his head to look at him. Merlyn continued to stare out to sea, expressionless. After a moment, Arthur turned his head back.

"I wasn't sure what to do. I needed advice."

A sea wave crashed before them, reflecting the light of the moon above and the fires behind.

"No, you didn't," Merlyn said in a monotone.

Arthur looked at him again. "What?"

Merlyn sighed. "You had made your decision. You called for me to waste time because you knew that by the time I was able to get to you, it would be too late."

Arthur turned to face Merlyn. Merlyn could feel tension and anger building in Arthur. Building to an explosion. Merlyn waited for the coming storm, continuing to stare out at the water. He could hear Arthur's breathing become quick and harsh.

Then Arthur blew air out of his lungs and turned back to the sea. The storm had passed.

Minutes passed.

"Yes. I did not realize it. But that is what I did."

"You did not want the responsibility of making the decision."

Arthur bent his head and raised his hands to his face. Was he the same as the Saxons? Killing the innocent when it was convenient and served his purpose? At least the Saxons didn't try to mask their intentions, as horrible as those intentions might be. Arthur, on the other hand, pretended he was standing on a moral high ground when he was not.

Merlyn spoke again, still staring straight out to sea. "Thus it is being a leader. Welcome an old friend, Arthur: the complexity of leadership." Turning to Arthur, he took a step and stretched out his hands to lay one on each of Arthur's shoulders. "Sometimes, it is too late to make a good decision. Sometimes, the only options *are* bad. And you will be inclined to pretend like it is not so, and find a way to rationalize it. And it will make sense to many people—most people—and they will understand."

"But *I* will know," Arthur whispered.

"Yes, you will. Or rather—" his mouth twisted up in a smile "—you will know when I am here to point it out."

Arthur snorted.

"And," Merlyn continued, "you will learn from it. You will learn to think ahead, and consider consequences, and options, and possibilities, and thus avoid the need to choose between two tragic options. But something like this *will* happen again. And perhaps in situations with more dire consequences than this."

Arthur raised his head and dropped his hands. "Is it a lack of character? Lack of faith?"

"Not at all, my son. It is human. What matters is how you respond *after* the failure."

He had killed women and children. No, it was not his policy. But he had done it to achieve his goal. Was he any better than his enemies?

Arthur's thoughts returned to the present as he washed his face in the basin of water in his tent. The water was now lukewarm. He lifted the towel from its hook and dried his face. *We criticize others for their actions, and we justify our own similar actions.*

Maybe Merlin was right. But how should one respond to such a sin? That dark night, near Caer Colum, Arthur had immediately turned away from the sea, mounted his horse, and rode through camp, quickly giving orders that any Saxons found alive were not to be harmed. His men were confused by this sudden change in orders, but followed his will. By the time the sun rose, the fires were out, and the dead had been dragged into a pile to be burned. Only two had been found alive: a male soldier who had been wounded and fallen into a garbage pit, and a young boy of about five years old, badly hurt when a structure had collapsed on him during the raid. He was so badly burned that no one could tell whether he was a Briton or a Saxon. Probably the former. Both died before dawn.

Arthur assembled his men and explained, as he had before, that it was not his policy to kill women or children in battle, no matter the circumstances. But this time he had allowed them to do so. He spoke to them. "Moral struggles come to us all: it is no sin," he said as he stood before them. "Even making the wrong decision is not a sin. But I failed you this day, and I failed to protect innocent people this day because I chose *not* to act. I did not have the courage to make a decision and live with the consequences. Moral courage may sometimes bring a wrong decision, but at least it stands up to be blamed or praised. I failed in this last night. Nevertheless, I confess it now, publicly."

Of course, his men did not believe he needed forgiveness. Arthur heard the talking and the rumors. Some thought such mistakes were simply part of war—how could he have known? Others believed his policy was too weak: Saxons kill British women and children, so if a few had to die to exterminate the Saxons, so be it. Still others seemed to understand that he had gone against a principle or taken the easy way out, but believed he was wrong to admit it publicly. To show a weakness through a public confession diminished his *gravitas*: it weakened him, and it weakened the army.

No matter. Arthur did not care. He was human and as weak as any other. He was bothered by the constant and growing stories about his power, intelligence, and fighting abilities. They took on a life of their own, and made him into a legendary figure that he knew did not exist, never had, and never would.

Arthur stirred himself once more to the present and began to dress. His clothes were still damp from having been cleaned last night. As he was buckling the leather jerkin around his upper body, another servant arrived with food and drink. Arthur sat on the bed and laced up his boots. The washing and the heat had revived him. The soreness was present, but manageable. The first few days of battle, the pain had been so acute. But there was also the excitement and anxiety of a new day of battle: the strategy and the personal skill involved, the unforeseen aspects of fighting that can only be spontaneously acted upon. There was anxiety every morning, of course: the sense of responsibility to his men, to his people, to his family. But now it just felt like a way of life. Like an old, tired liturgy which droned on and on, day after day, week after week. Waking, thinking, water, dress, food, assembly, marching, fighting, chaos, dusk, trudging, collapse, food, discussion, tent, undressing, exhaustion, collapsing, and sleep. He knew there was more to life out there somewhere, but it was a dim memory. Green rolling hills covered with heather, sprawling farms, and sheep dotting the lands. The warmth of family and friends, the security of his own home and land in Caerleon, the comfort of a home fire. Leisure time, walking along the shore of the Bristol Channel with Gwenhwyfar, hunting with Cay and Merlyn and Powys in Cerniw. All a dream now. His life was only physical and mental exhaustion, strategy and planning, fighting and leading—the battlefield, this camp, this tent. During the second week of the battle, he was sick of his tent. He hated the look of it, the smell of it. Now it merely his world. This tent and the battlefield. Nothing else existed.

He stood up and walked to the table, peering into the metal pan the servant had set there. A few slices of roasted boar, three roasted eggs, and five small oatcakes. Beside the pan was a mug of ale. He lifted the mug and took a deep draught. It was stale, of course, but it enlivened him and brought him further awake as the alcohol warmed his throat and belly. The sensation spread through his torso. Still holding the mug, he took a slice of meat with his other hand and chewed off a piece. It was almost as good as it was last night, even cold. Arthur always insisted that he be given no special food; he ate the same as everyone else in camp.

Powys returned as he was eating one of the eggs. "Merlyn said will be along shortly, my lord. He had something to attend to."

Arthur wiped his mouth with his sleeve, the smell of sweat and blood drawing his attention briefly. He held his forearm before him and stared at it morosely. "He always has some secret thing to attend to," he said absently.

"He is a druid."

Arthur dropped his arm and looked up at him. "How are the men this morning?"

"About the same. Ninety-five dead, including those wounded who did not survive the night. We have two hundred and forty-five new wounded, sixty-three of which will not be able to fight today. Twenty-three previously infirm will return to battle today."

"If those numbers hold true on a daily basis, we can keep this up for some time."

"Indeed. We are doing better than expected. I am willing to say we are winning, though I do not have the enemy numbers. Scouts have not returned yet."

Arthur took a long drink of ale, draining the mug. He set it down with a bang. "'Numbers'," he said forcefully.

"My lord?"

Arthur sighed and made a face. "I said, 'if we keep up these *numbers*.' Men are not numbers. They are people. Living beings. With loves, hates, families, dreams, fears."

Powys looked as if he did not know what to say. "Yes, my lord."

They stood in silence for a while. Arthur stirred suddenly. "Time to prepare." He walked to the table and picked up his greaves. The leather was cool from the cold night. Powys came and took them from him. He bent and placed them on Arthur's shins, wrapping the straps and buckling them tightly. "Okay?" he asked, looking up. "Yes, that is fine."

Powys then picked up Arthur's short mail shirt and held it so that Arthur could bend his head and allow Powys to place it over his head and around his neck. Arthur then pulled it down over his torso and arranged it properly. As he was doing so, the tent flap opened, and Merlyn strode in with a swirl of cloth and leather attended by the feel and smell of cold air.

"Ah, good. You are looking much better now. The sun peeks over the Tor Pen in about fifteen minutes. The men are assembling." He strode over to the table and picked through some of Arthur's leftovers, selecting a small piece of meat, a portion which was dried and burned, and put it in his mouth. Arthur held out his arms so that Powys could buckle his leather forearm guards. He watched Merlyn as he did so.

"Merlyn, I have been thinking about the maneuver we performed on the first day, when the Fourteenth circled behind the Silvan Wood and worked their way through to the Saxon's left flank. Could we do that again, maybe with the Sixteenth? Would the Saxons be prepared for it? It has been three weeks."

"Since we have done it once, it is unlikely they will be taken completely by surprise. And they may have scouts in the Wood, to watch for a repeat of such tactics. I do not think they would spare enough for a fighting force, though." His brow furrowed. "The battle has moved slightly in the direction of our camp, as you know. Our soldiers would come out of the wood about a half a mile behind the enemy flank this time, instead of right at it. The Saxon rearguard would assuredly spot them as they advanced from out of the woods."

"Yes. I was thinking of having them exit through the south end of the wood, farther back, so they would come out behind that line of downs where the enemy rearguard could not see them."

Merlyn raised his eyebrows. "You want to raid their camp while they are at battle?"

Powys had finished dressing Arthur for battle. The king walked to his bed, bent down, and picked up his dirk from the floor. He stuck it through a loop on the left side of his wide belt. He turned to face Merlyn and took a deep breath. "Yes. But not to kill and burn. To take their food supplies and cooking utensils."

Merlyn smiled. "A strange battle tactic. Most would want slaves and booty. You want food and dishes."

Arthur scowled at him. "No. I want to make camping difficult for them so that they will retreat. We can then chase them, and we do well nipping at the edges of an army and wearing them down. Fewer casualties for us. We are a better guerrilla force than a field army."

"Yes, I know what you intend: I was poking at you. I also know that you are worried that some of their wounded at their camp hospital might be killed. Defenseless. And you even wonder if they might have some women, or even children, as we have found occasionally in past skirmishes the last few months."

Arthur looked steadily at him. "Merlyn, I need to defeat the Saxons. I need to save my people and their homes. I must keep Britons free from the fear of marauders. And I know you will say that war is full of moral dilemmas, and that 'might makes right' or that 'a right end justifies almost any means.' And you know that I agree with you. I know it from experience. The choices I make in horrific situations will not always feel good. I want things nice and clean. But life is not like that, I have learned. We are all sullied. We are all unclean."

Merlyn looked at him with an expression of part amusement and part pride. He raised his eyebrows. "Yes?"

"I don't know. I mean, I do know. We need to win. And we need to make difficult choices, and some of the choices we make may be wrong. Some of the choices *I* make may be wrong. And yes, it is true, I feel guilt over my past decisions in which I chose wrongly. Even the ones in which I tried to do right, but unintended consequences caused me guilt."

Arthur sighed and looked away from Merlyn. "But that I can handle. We all have guilt if we are honest. Making tough decisions and living with the consequences is one thing—but rationalizing the bad decisions is another. Making a choice between two awful options is one thing—but taking the easy way out merely to soothe the conscience is another."

He looked firmly back at Merlyn. "I will win this war. But not at the cost of losing our souls. Even if it costs us our lives."

Merlyn had quit smiling. "Many would disagree, Arthur. Many would say that it is not a matter of losing your soul. The Saxons are evil, and whatever it takes, you should rid this land of them. By whatever means necessary. Might makes right. So many would say."

"And you say?"

"I agree with you, of course. Life's most important tasks often seem to be protecting oneself, one's land, one's own kin, and especially protecting those who cannot protect themselves. But there is something more essential than those things, something that rises above our lives and our livelihood. We will someday stand in the Otherworld and look back on this world. What will we think then? What would we say to our younger selves and to those who come after? *That* matters far more than what your friends and enemies say about you today and tomorrow." He paused and gave a conspiratorial wink. "Or what history will say about you."

"History," Arthur snorted. He stood silently for a moment. He looked over at Powys, who had been standing quietly, watching the two men. One old, one young. One a warrior-druid, the other a warrior-king. One with the aura of deep and ancient wisdom, the other with the aura of a great and compassionate leader.

Merlyn broke the silence. "But keep this in mind, Arthur: do not mistake cowardice for compassion and 'soul.' It often takes more courage to do the right thing because of its difficult consequences."

Arthur turned to Powys. "Brief Captain Alain of the Sixteenth. He is to prepare his men for a special mission. Light armor, no supplies. Quick and silent, they are to be. I'll give them details at the assembly."

"Aye, sir." He waited.

"That is all, Powys. I will be there shortly. *Pax robiscom*."

"And you, my lord." Powys turned and left the tent. Arthur turned back to Merlyn. "Are we ready? Am I forgetting anything?"

Merlyn smiled. "Most assuredly, you are forgetting something. We all do. But we are as ready as we can be at this moment."

"Your encouragement is always overwhelming, my friend. Are you ever blindly optimistic?"

"Never. I play my role. Optimism, be it blind or sighted, I leave to others."

Arthur stood looking at him for a moment, then smiled grimly. "Yes, indeed. We all have our roles. Blessed are you that know yours so clearly."

Merlyn winced. "It is not always a blessing." He turned. "It is time. I will leave you to your meditation and see you at the grounds shortly."

Merlyn left the tent. The sound of his feet crunching on the cold ground outside was clear in the still morning, fading away as he went from the tent. It became quiet. So quiet that Arthur could hear the slight fluffing sound of the candles burning. He stood still for a few moments, relishing the silence and the stillness. Soon, he would be surrounded by the deathly noise of voices, clanging metal, and booted feet on hard ground. Soon there would be no time to reflect, to stand still, or to breathe slowly. And then it would end again for that day, and he would come back here with another period of horror finished, God willing. The cycle would start again. When would it be over? A few days? Weeks? How would it end? A withdrawal by the enemy? A slow petering out as there are fewer and fewer left to continue? A victory and rout by his own—or by the enemy?

Maybe it would end with his own death.

That thought brought a great desire to give up again. Just to give up: what a relief it would be. The world would go on its way. History, as Merlyn said, would make its own judgments—but Arthur would no longer care. Possibly nothing would change overmuch. They say he is the king of Briton, the anointed one of God, and that he has a special role at a special time. Many unusual events *had* taken place that bore out the truth of that: his unusual birth, the finding of the Sword, the prophecies of the Lady of the Lake, and so on. Yet this did not keep Arthur from frequently questioning it all. And now, the weariness and the pain…would it be so bad if the Saxons triumphed? If they took over all of Briton? So what if one people replaced another? It had happened many times in human history. Many people would die horrible deaths. The Celts of Briton would be no longer. Would it make all that much difference in the larger march of history?

He was so tired mentally, physically, and emotionally. How much more could one take? Was this not the description of hell? Day after day, facing the unknown, the fear, the pain, the exhaustion?

With great effort, Arthur shook his head, in an attempt to shake away those debilitating thoughts. He walked to the corner of the tent where the cross stood. Kneeling down on one knee, he crossed himself. After reciting the Lord's Prayer, he looked up to the top of the tent.

"*In nomine Patris, et Filii, et Spiritus Sancti… Amen.*"

He rose slowly, the leather of his armor creaking in the silence, mixed with the small and muffled clinks of the chain mail rubbing together. *Will I hear these sounds again tomorrow morning?* He went to the candles, cupping a hand behind, and blew them out one by one. The white smoke swirled up in the cold air from the black wicks, the pungent smell bringing back memories of home when Gwenhwyfar would blow out the candles in their chamber at night. *Will I experience that again someday?*

Taking up his sword with his left hand, just below the hilt, he held it before him, his arm straight out. The heft was great, so much so that his arm strained to hold it so. The metal glinted from the slight bit of daylight that filtered into the darkened tent. He reached out his right hand and took the hilt, spinning the sword around upright and holding it out, pointing slightly forward, cupping his left hand around his right on the hilt. *Such a familiar feel.* The sword, almost as famous as himself, had been a constant companion since just before he was a man. *How many more days shall I wield it?*

He sighed. He dropped the point of the sword to the ground. Did he really have the strength to go out again, to fight again, to hurt again, and to pretend to be the powerful, strong, confident leader that all expected of him—and needed of him?

No. I do not have that strength. But, God be with me, I must. He breathed deeply, and, hefting Excalibur once again, he sheathed the mighty sword with a loud clang.

How I long for just one day with no fear, no pain, no suffering.

Surely, one day, his body, mind, and heart would refuse to cooperate. His body would collapse, his mind would rebel, his heart would give up. They would scream, *no more!*

But not today.

He stepped to the flap of the tent and threw it open just as the sun rose over Tor Pen.

About the Author

If you enjoyed from this book, please consider posting an online review. The author thanks you in advance.

Markus McDowell is an author and editor of fiction and nonfiction in multiple genres. He is the author of *Nuff Sed: A Novel of Desert Steve*, *To and Fro Upon the Earth: A Novel, Mortals As They Walk, Onesimus: A Novel of Christianity in the Roman Empire*, and two other short story collections, *The Sky Over Chaos* and *So Deep in Shadow,* as well as several nonfiction books in law, theology, and literature in the ancient world. He lives in California on a boat and travels extensively.

Visit the author's website at
https://markusmcdowell.com/

Join Team Markus
https://markusmcdowell.com/newsletter/

Follow on social media:
Instagram: https://www.instagram.com/doctormarkus_au-thor/
Facebook: https://www.facebook.com/MarkusMcDowell-Author/
X: https://x.com/markusmcdowell
Goodreads: http://goodreads.com/author/show/8404913.Markus_McDowell

About the Publisher

Sulis International Press publishes select fiction and nonfiction in a variety of genres under four imprints:

- Riversong Books (fiction)
- Sulis Press (general nonfiction)
- Keledei Publications (spirituality)
- Sulis Academic Press (academic works)

For more, visit the website at
https://sulisinternational.com

Subscribe to the newsletter at
https://sulisinternational.com/subscribe/

Follow on social media
https://www.facebook.com/SulisInternational
https://twitter.com/Sulis_Intl
https://www.pinterest.com/Sulis_Intl/
https://www.instagram.com/sulis_international/